Algernon Charles Swinburne

Poems and Ballads

Third Series

Algernon Charles Swinburne

Poems and Ballads
Third Series

ISBN/EAN: 9783337063672

Printed in Europe, USA, Canada, Australia, Japan

Cover: Foto ©Andreas Hilbeck / pixelio.de

More available books at **www.hansebooks.com**

POEMS AND BALLADS

THIRD SERIES

BY

ALGERNON CHARLES SWINBURNE

TENTH IMPRESSION

LONDON

CHATTO & WINDUS

1910

TO

WILLIAM BELL SCOTT

POET AND PAINTER

I DEDICATE THESE POEMS

IN MEMORY OF MANY YEARS

CONTENTS

MARCH: AN ODE.

1887.

I.

ERE frost-flower and snow-blossom faded and fell, and
the splendour of winter had passed out of sight,
The ways of the woodlands were fairer and stranger than
dreams that fulfil us in sleep with delight ;
The breath of the mouths of the winds had hardened on
tree-tops and branches that glittered and swayed
Such wonders and glories of blossomlike snow or of frost
that outlightens all flowers till it fade
That the sea was not lovelier than here was the land, nor
the night than the day, nor the day than the night,

Nor the winter sublimer with storm than the spring : such

    mirth had the madness and might in thee made,

March, master of winds, bright minstrel and marshal of

    storms that enkindle the season they smite.

II.

And now that the rage of thy rapture is satiate with revel

    and ravin and spoil of the snow,

And the branches it brightened are broken, and shattered

    the tree-tops that only thy wrath could lay low,

How should not thy lovers rejoice in thee, leader and

    lord of the year that exults to be born

So strong in thy strength and so glad of thy gladness whose

    laughter puts winter and sorrow to scorn ?

Thou hast shaken the snows from thy wings, and the frost

    on thy forehead is molten : thy lips are aglow

As a lover's that kindle with kissing, and earth, with her

    raiment and tresses yet wasted and torn,

Takes breath as she smiles in the grasp of thy passion to

    feel through her spirit the sense of thee flow.

III.

Fain, fain would we see but again for an hour what the
    wind and the sun have dispelled and consumed,

Those full deep swan-soft feathers of snow with whose
    luminous burden the branches implumed

Hung heavily, curved as a half-bent bow, and fledged not
    as birds are, but petalled as flowers,

Each tree-top and branchlet a pinnacle jewelled and
    carved, or a fountain that shines as it showers,

But fixed as a fountain is fixed not, and wrought not to
    last till by time or by tempest entombed,

As a pinnacle carven and gilded of men : for the date of
    its doom is no more than an hour's,

One hour of the sun's when the warm wind wakes him to
    wither the snow-flowers that froze as they bloomed.

IV.

As the sunshine quenches the snowshine ; as April sub-
    dues thee, and yields up his kingdom to May ;

So time overcomes the regret that is born of delight as
it passes in passion away,

And leaves but a dream for desire to rejoice in or mourn
for with tears or thanksgivings ; but thou,

Bright god that art gone from us, maddest and gladdest
of months, to what goal hast thou gone from us now ?

For somewhere surely the storm of thy laughter that
lightens, the beat of thy wings that play,

Must flame as a fire through the world, and the heavens
that we know not rejoice in thee : surely thy brow

Hath lost not its radiance of empire, thy spirit the joy
that impelled it on quest as for prey.

V.

Are thy feet on the ways of the limitless waters, thy wings
on the winds of the waste north sea ?

Are the fires of the false north dawn over heavens where
summer is stormful and strong like thee

Now bright in the sight of thine eyes ? are the bastions
of icebergs assailed by the blast of thy breath ?

Is it March with the wild north world when April is
  waning? the word that the changed year saith,
Is it echoed to northward with rapture of passion reiterate
  from spirits triumphant as we
Whose hearts were uplift at the blast of thy clarions as
  men's rearisen from a sleep that was death
And kindled to life that was one with the world's and with
  thine? hast thou set not the whole world free?

VI.

For the breath of thy lips is freedom, and freedom's the
  sense of thy spirit, the sound of thy song,
Glad god of the north-east wind, whose heart is as high
  as the hands of thy kingdom are strong,
Thy kingdom whose empire is terror and joy, twin-featured
  and fruitful of births divine,
Days lit with the flame of the lamps of the flowers, and
  nights that are drunken with dew for wine,
And sleep not for joy of the stars that deepen and quicken,
  a denser and fierier throng,

And the world that thy breath bade whiten and tremble
　　rejoices at heart as they strengthen and shine,
And earth gives thanks for the glory bequeathed her, and
　　knows of thy reign that it wrought not wrong.

VII.

Thy spirit is quenched not, albeit we behold not thy face
　　in the crown of the steep sky's arch,
And the bold first buds of the whin wax golden, and
　　witness arise of the thorn and the larch :
Wild April, enkindled to laughter and storm by the kiss
　　of the wildest of winds that blow,
Calls loud on his brother for witness ; his hands that
　　were laden with blossom are sprinkled with snow,
And his lips breathe winter, and laugh, and relent ; and
　　the live woods feel not the frost's flame parch ;
For the flame of the spring that consumes not but quickens
　　is felt at the heart of the forest aglow,
And the sparks that enkindled and fed it were strewn from
　　the hands of the gods of the winds of March.

THE COMMONWEAL

1887.

I.

EIGHT hundred years and twenty-one
  Have shone and sunken since the land
  Whose name is freedom bore such brand
As marks a captive, and the sun
  Beheld her fettered hand.

II.

But ere dark time had shed as rain
  Or sown on sterile earth as seed
  That bears no fruit save tare and weed
An age and half an age again,
  She rose on Runnymede.

III.

Out of the shadow, starlike still,
  She rose up radiant in her right,
  And spake, and put to fear and flight
The lawless rule of awless will
  That pleads no right save might.

IV.

Nor since hath England ever borne
  The burden laid on subject lands,
  The rule that curbs and binds all hands
Save one, and marks for servile scorn
  The heads it bows and brands.

V.

A commonweal arrayed and crowned
  With gold and purple, girt with steel
  At need, that foes must fear or feel,
We find her, as our fathers found,
  Earth's lordliest commonweal.

VI.

And now that fifty years are flown

    Since in a maiden's hand the sign

    Of empire that no seas confine

First as a star to seaward shone,

    We see their record shine.

VII.

A troubled record, foul and fair,

    A simple record and serene,

    Inscribes for praise a blameless queen,

For praise and blame an age of care

    And change and ends unseen.

VIII.

Hope, wide of eye and wild of wing,

    Rose with the sundawn of a reign

    Whose grace should make the rough ways plain,

And fill the worn old world with spring,

    And heal its heart of pain.

IX.

Peace was to be on earth ; men's hope
  Was holier than their fathers had,
  Their wisdom not more wise than glad :
They saw the gates of promise ope,
  And heard what love's lips bade.

X.

Love armed with knowledge, winged and wise,
  Should hush the wind of war, and see,
  They said, the sun of days to be
Bring round beneath serener skies
  A stormless jubilee.

XI.

Time, in the darkness unbeholden
  That hides him from the sight of fear
  And lets but dreaming hope draw near,
Smiled and was sad to hear such golden
  Strains hail the all-golden year.

XII.

Strange clouds have risen between, and wild

Red stars of storm that lit the abyss

Wherein fierce fraud and violence kiss

And mock such promise as beguiled

The fiftieth year from this.

XIII.

War upon war, change after change,

Hath shaken thrones and towers to dust,

And hopes austere and faiths august

Have watched in patience stern and strange

Men's works unjust and just.

XIV.

As from some Alpine watch-tower's portal

Night, living yet, looks forth for dawn,

So from time's mistier mountain lawn

The spirit of man, in trust immortal,

Yearns toward a hope withdrawn.

xv.

The morning comes not, yet the night
    Wanes, and men's eyes win strength to see
    Where twilight is, where light shall be
When conquered wrong and conquering right
    Acclaim a world set free.

xvi.

Calm as our mother-land, the mother
    Of faith and freedom, pure and wise,
    Keeps watch beneath unchangeful skies,
When hath she watched the woes of other
    Strange lands with alien eyes?

xvii.

Calm as she stands alone, what nation
    Hath lacked an alms from English hands?
    What exiles from what stricken lands
Have lacked the shelter of the station
    Where higher than all she stands?

XVIII.

Though time discrown and change dismantle

　The pride of thrones and towers that frown,

　How should they bring her glories down—

The sea cast round her like a mantle,

　The sea-cloud like a crown?

XIX.

The sea, divine as heaven and deathless,

　Is hers, and none but only she

　Hath learnt the sea's word, none but we

Her children hear in heart the breathless

　Bright watchword of the sea.

XX.

Heard not of others, or misheard

　Of many a land for many a year,

　The watchword Freedom fails not here

Of hearts that witness if the word

　Find faith in England's ear.

XXI.

She, first to love the light, and daughter

　　Incarnate of the northern dawn,

　　She, round whose feet the wild waves fawn

When all their wrath of warring water

　　Sounds like a babe's breath drawn,

XXII.

How should not she best know, love best,

　　And best of all souls understand

　　The very soul of freedom, scanned

Far off, sought out in darkling quest

　　By men at heart unmanned ?

XXIII.

They climb and fall, ensnared, enshrouded,

　　By mists of words and toils they set

　　To take themselves, till fierce regret

Grows mad with shame, and all their clouded

　　Red skies hang sunless yet.

XXIV.

But us the sun, not wholly risen

   Nor equal now for all, illumes

   With more of light than cloud that looms ;

Of light that leads forth souls from prison

   And breaks the seals of tombs.

XXV.

Did not her breasts who reared us rear

   Him who took heaven in hand, and weighed

   Bright world with world in balance laid ?

What Newton's might could make not clear

   Hath Darwin's might not made?

XXVI.

The forces of the dark dissolve,

   The doorways of the dark are broken :

   The word that casts out night is spoken,

And whence the springs of things evolve

   Light born of night bears token.

XXVII.

She, loving light for light's sake only,

And truth for only truth's, and song

For song's sake and the sea's, how long

Hath she not borne the world her lonely

Witness of right and wrong?

XXVIII.

From light to light her eyes imperial

Turn, and require the further light,

More perfect than the sun's in sight,

Till star and sun seem all funereal

Lamps of the vaulted night.

XXIX.

She gazes till the strenuous soul

Within the rapture of her eyes

Creates or bids awake, arise,

The light she looks for, pure and whole

And worshipped of the wise.

XXX.

Such sons are hers, such radiant hands
　　Have borne abroad her lamp of old,
　　Such mouths of honey-dropping gold
Have sent across all seas and lands
　　Her fame as music rolled.

XXXI.

As music made of rolling thunder
　　That hurls through heaven its heart sublime,
　　Its heart of joy, in charging chime,
So ring the songs that round and under
　　Her temple surge and climb.

XXXII.

A temple not by men's hands builded,
　　But moulded of the spirit, and wrought
　　Of passion and imperious thought ;
With light beyond all sunlight gilded,
　　Whereby the sun seems nought.

XXXIII.

Thy shrine, our mother, seen for fairer

Than even thy natural face, made fair

With kisses of thine April air

Even now, when spring thy banner-bearer

Took up thy sign to bear ;

XXXIV.

Thine annual sign from heaven's own arch

Given of the sun's hand into thine,

To rear and cheer each wildwood shrine

But now laid waste by wild-winged March,

March, mad with wind like wine.

XXXV.

From all thy brightening downs whereon

The windy seaward whin-flower shows

Blossom whose pride strikes pale the rose

Forth is the golden watchword gone

Whereat the world's face glows.

XXXVI.

Thy quickening woods rejoice and ring

    Till earth seems glorious as the sea :

    With yearning love too glad for glee

The world's heart quivers toward the spring

    As all our hearts toward thee.

XXXVII.

Thee, mother, thee, our queen, who givest

    Assurance to the heavens most high

    And earth whereon her bondsmen sigh

That by the sea's grace while thou livest

    Hope shall not wholly die.

XXXVIII.

That while thy free folk hold the van

    Of all men, and the sea-spray shed

    As dew more heavenly on thy head

Keeps bright thy face in sight of man,

    Man's pride shall drop not dead.

XXXIX.

A pride more pure than humblest prayer,

  More wise than wisdom born of doubt,

  Girds for thy sake men's hearts about

With trust and triumph that despair

  And fear may cast not out.

XL.

Despair may wring men's hearts, and fear

  Bow down their heads to kiss the dust,

  Where patriot memories rot and rust,

And change makes faint a nation's cheer,

  And faith yields up her trust.

XLI.

Not here this year have true men known,

  Not here this year may true men know,

  That brand of shame-compelling woe

Which bids but brave men shrink or groan

  And lays but honour low.

XLII.

The strong spring wind blows notes of praise,

 And hallowing pride of heart, and cheer

 Unchanging, toward all true men here

Who hold the trust of ancient days

 High as of old this year.

XLIII.

The days that made thee great are dead ;

 The days that now must keep thee great

 Lie not in keeping of thy fate ;

In thine they lie, whose heart and head

 Sustain thy charge of state.

XLIV.

No state so proud, no pride so just,

 The sun, through clouds at sunrise curled

 Or clouds across the sunset whirled,

Hath sight of, nor has man such trust

 As thine in all the world.

XLV.

Each hour that sees the sunset's crest
  Make bright thy shores ere day decline
  Sees dawn the sun on shores of thine,
Sees west as east and east as west
  On thee their sovereign shine.

XLVI.

The sea's own heart must needs wax proud
  To have borne the world a child like thee.
  What birth of earth might ever be
Thy sister?   Time, a wandering cloud,
  Is sunshine on thy sea.

XLVII.

Change mars not her ; and thee, our mother,
  What change that irks or moves thee mars ?
  What shock that shakes? what chance that jars?
Time gave thee, as he gave none other,
  A station like a star's.

XLVIII.

The storm that shrieks, the wind that wages

    War with the wings of hopes that climb

    Too high toward heaven in doubt sublime,

Assail not thee, approved of ages

    The towering crown of time.

XLIX.

Toward thee this year thy children turning

    With souls uplift of changeless cheer

    Salute with love that casts out fear,

With hearts for beacons round thee burning,

    The token of this year.

L.

With just and sacred jubilation

    Let earth sound answer to the sea

    For witness, blown on winds as free,

How England, how her crowning nation,

    Acclaims this jubilee.

THE ARMADA.

1588 : 1888.

I.

I.

ENGLAND, mother born of seamen, daughter fostered of
the sea,

Mother more beloved than all who bear not all their
children free,

Reared and nursed and crowned and cherished by the
sea-wind and the sun,

Sweetest land and strongest, face most fair and mightiest heart in one,

Stands not higher than when the centuries known of
earth were less by three,

When the strength that struck the whole world pale
fell back from hers undone.

II.

At her feet were the heads of her foes bowed down, and
the strengths of the storm of them stayed,

And the hearts that were touched not with mercy with
terror were touched and amazed and affrayed :

Yea, hearts that had never been molten with pity were
molten with fear as with flame,

And the priests of the Godhead whose temple is hell,
and his heart is of iron and fire,

And the swordsmen that served and the seamen that
sped them, whom peril could tame not or tire,

Were as foam on the winds of the waters of England
which tempest can tire not or tame.

III.

They were girded about with thunder, and lightning came
forth of the rage of their strength,

And the measure that measures the wings of the storm
was the breadth of their force and the length :

And the name of their might was Invincible, covered
and clothed with the terror of God ;

With his wrath were they winged, with his love were they
fired, with the speed of his winds were they shod ;

With his soul were they filled, in his trust were they com-
forted : grace was upon them as night,

And faith as the blackness of darkness : the fume of
their balefires was fair in his sight,

The reek of them sweet as a savour of myrrh in his
nostrils : the world that he made,

Theirs was it by gift of his servants : the wind, if they
spake in his name, was afraid,

And the sun was a shadow before it, the stars were
astonished with fear of it : fire

Went up to them, fed with men living, and lit of men's
hands for a shrine or a pyre ;

And the east and the west wind scattered their ashes
abroad, that his name should be blest

Of the tribes of the chosen whose blessings are curses
from uttermost east unto west.

II.

I.

Hell for Spain, and heaven for England,—God to God, and man to man,—

Met confronted, light with darkness, life with death : since time began,

Never earth nor sea beheld so great a stake before them set,

Save when Athens hurled back Asia from the lists wherein they met;

Never since the sands of ages through the glass of history ran

Saw the sun in heaven a lordlier day than this that lights us yet.

II.

For the light that abides upon England, the glory that rests on her godlike name,

The pride that is love and the love that is faith, a perfume
  dissolved in flame,

  Took fire from the dawn of the fierce July when fleets
  were scattered as foam

And squadrons as flakes of spray; when galleon and
  galliass that shadowed the sea

Were swept from her waves like shadows that pass with
  the clouds they fell from, and she

  Laughed loud to the wind as it gave to her keeping
  the glories of Spain and Rome.

III.

Three hundred summers have fallen as leaves by the
  storms in their season thinned,

Since northward the war-ships of Spain came sheer up
  the way of the south-west wind :

Where the citadel cliffs of England are flanked with bastions of serpentine,

Far off to the windward loomed their hulls, an hundred
  and twenty-nine,

All filled full of the war, full-fraught with battle and
  charged with bale ;

Then store-ships weighted with cannon ; and all were an
  hundred and fifty sail.

The measureless menace of darkness anhungered with
  hope to prevail upon light,

The shadow of death made substance, the present and
  visible spirit of night,

Came, shaped as a waxing or waning moon that rose
  with the fall of day,

To the channel where couches the Lion in guard of the
  gate of the lustrous bay.

Fair England, sweet as the sea that shields her, and pure
  as the sea from stain,

Smiled, hearing hardly for scorn that stirred her the
  menace of saintly Spain.

III.

I.

'They that ride over ocean wide with hempen bridle and
　　horse of tree,'
How shall they in the darkening day of wrath and an-
　　guish and fear go free?
How shall these that have curbed the seas not feel his
　　bridle who made the sea?

God shall bow them and break them now: for what is
　　man in the Lord God's sight?
Fear shall shake them, and shame shall break, and all
　　the noon of their pride be night:
These that sinned shall the ravening wind of doom bring
　　under, and judgment smite.

England broke from her neck the yoke, and rent the
　　fetter. and mocked the rod:

Shrines of old that she decked with gold she turned to
dust, to the dust she trod :

What is she, that the wind and sea should fight beside
her, and war with God?

Lo, the cloud of his ships that crowd her channel's inlet
with storm sublime,

Darker far than the tempests are that sweep the skies of
her northmost clime ;

Huge and dense as the walls that fence the secret darkness of unknown time.

Mast on mast as a tower goes past, and sail by sail as a
cloud's wing spread ;

Fleet by fleet, as the throngs whose feet keep time with
death in his dance of dread ;

Galleons dark as the helmsman's bark of old that ferried
to hell the dead.

Squadrons proud as their lords, and loud with tramp of
soldiers and chant of priests ;

Slaves there told by the thousandfold, made fast in
    bondage as herded beasts ;
Lords and slaves that the sweet free waves shall feed on,
    satiate with funeral feasts.

Nay, not so shall it be, they know ; their priests have said
    it ; can priesthood lie ?
God shall keep them, their God shall sleep not : peril
    and evil shall pass them by :
Nay, for these are his children ; seas and winds shall bid
    not his children die.

II.

So they boast them, the monstrous host whose menace
    mocks at the dawn : and here
They that wait at the wild sea's gate, and watch the dark-
    ness of doom draw near,
How shall they in their evil day sustain the strength of
    their hearts for fear ?

Full July in the fervent sky sets forth her twentieth of

    changing morns :

Winds fall mild that of late waxed wild : no presage

    whispers or wails or warns :

Far to west on the bland sea's breast a sailing crescent

    uprears her horns.

Seven wide miles the serene sea smiles between them

    stretching from rim to rim :

Soft they shine, but a darker sign should bid not hope or

    belief wax dim :

God's are these men, and not the sea's : their trust is set

    not on her but him.

God's ? but who is the God whereto the prayers and

    incense of these men rise ?

What is he, that the wind and sea should fear him, quelled

    by his sunbright eyes ?

What, that men should return again, and hail him Lord

    of the servile skies ?

III.   D

Hell's own flame at his heavenly name leaps higher and
laughs, and its gulfs rejoice :

Plague and death from his baneful breath take life and
lighten, and praise his choice :

Chosen are they to devour for prey the tribes that hear not
and fear his voice.

Ay, but we that the wind and sea gird round with shelter
of storms and waves

Know not him that ye worship, grim as dreams that
quicken from dead men's graves :

God is one with the sea, the sun, the land that nursed us,
the love that saves.

Love whose heart is in ours, and part of all things noble
and all things fair ;

Sweet and free as the circling sea, sublime and kind as
the fostering air ;

Pure of shame as is England's name, whose crowns to
come are as crowns that were.

IV.

I.

But the Lord of darkness, the God whose love is a flaming
    fire,

The master whose mercy fulfils wide hell till its torturers
    tire,

He shall surely have heed of his **servants** who serve him
    for love, not hire.

They shall fetter the wing of the wind whose pinions are
    plumed with foam :

For now shall thy horn be exalted, and now shall thy
    bolt strike home ;

Yea, now shall thy kingdom come, Lord God of the priests
    of Rome.

They shall cast thy curb on the waters, and bridle the
 waves of the sea :
They shall say to her, Peace, be still : and stillness and
 peace shall be :
And the winds and the storms shall hear them, and
 tremble, and worship thee.

Thy breath shall darken the morning, and wither the
 mounting sun ;
And the daysprings, frozen and fettered, shall know thee,
 and cease to run ;
The heart of the world shall feel thee, and die, and thy
 will be done.

The spirit of man that would sound thee, and search out
 causes of things,
Shall shrink and subside and praise thee : and wisdom,
 with plume-plucked wings,
Shall cower at thy feet and confess thee, that none may
 fathom thy springs.

The fountains of song that await but the wind of an April
to be

To burst the bonds of the winter, and speak with the
sound of a sea,

The blast of thy mouth shall quench them : and song
shall be only of thee.

The days that are dead shall quicken, the seasons that
were shall return ;

And the streets and the pastures of England, the woods
that burgeon and yearn,

Shall be whitened with ashes of women and children and
men that burn.

For the mother shall burn with the babe sprung forth of
her womb in fire,

And bride with bridegroom, and brother with sister, and
son with sire ;

And the noise of the flames shall be sweet in thine ears
as the sound of a lyre.

Yea, so shall thy kingdom be stablished, and so shall the

signs of it be :

And the world shall know, and the wind shall speak, and

the sun shall see,

That these are the works of thy servants, whose works

bear witness to thee.

II.

But the dusk of the day falls fruitless, whose light should

have lit them on :

Sails flash through the gloom to shoreward, eclipsed as

the sun that shone :

And the west wind wakes with dawn, and the hope that

was here is gone.

Around they wheel and around, two knots to the Spaniard's

one,

The wind-swift warriors of England, who shoot as with

shafts of the sun,

With fourfold shots for the Spaniard's, that spare not till

day be done.

And the wind with the sundown sharpens, and hurtles the
ships to the lee,

And Spaniard on Spaniard smites, and shatters, and
yields ; and we,

Ere battle begin, stand lords of the battle, acclaimed of
the sea.

And the day sweeps round to the nightward ; and heavy
and hard the waves

Roll in on the herd of the hurtling galleons ; and masters
and slaves

Reel blind in the grasp of the dark strong wind that shall
dig their graves.

For the sepulchres hollowed and shaped of the wind in
the swerve of the seas,

The graves that gape for their pasture, and laugh, thrilled
through by the breeze,

The sweet soft merciless waters, await and are fain of
these.

As the hiss of a Python heaving in menace of doom to be

They hear through the clear night round them, whose
hours are as clouds that flee,

The whisper of tempest sleeping, the heave and the hiss
of the sea.

But faith is theirs, and with faith are they girded and
helmed and shod :

Invincible are they, almighty, elect for a sword and a
rod ;

Invincible even as their God is omnipotent, infinite,
God.

In him is their strength, who have sworn that his glory
shall wax not dim :

In his name are their war-ships hallowed as mightiest of
all that swim :

The men that shall cope with these, and conquer, shall
cast out him.

In him is the trust of their hearts ; the desire of their eyes

is he ;

The light of their ways, made lightning for men that

would fain be free :

Earth's hosts are with them, and with them is heaven :

but with us is the sea.   .

V.

I.

And a day and a night pass over ;

And the heart of their chief swells high ;

For England, the warrior, the rover,

Whose banners on all winds fly,

Soul-stricken, he saith, by the shadow of death, holds off

him, and draws not nigh.

And the wind and the dawn together

Make in from the gleaming east :

And fain of the wild glad weather
   As famine is fain of feast,
And fain of the fight, forth sweeps in its might the host
   of the Lord's high priest.

And lightly before the breeze
   The ships of his foes take wing :
   Are they scattered, the lords of the seas ?
   Are they broken, the foes of the king ?
And ever now higher as a mounting fire the hopes of the
   Spaniard spring.

And a windless night comes down :
   And a breezeless morning, bright
   With promise of praise to crown
   The close of the crowning fight,
Leaps up as the foe's heart leaps, and glows with lustrous
   rapture of light.

And stinted of gear for battle

    The ships of the sea's folk lie,

Unwarlike, herded as cattle,

    Six miles from the foeman's eye

That fastens as flame on the sight of them tame and

offenceless, and ranged as to die.

Surely the souls in them quail,

    They are stricken and withered at heart,

When in on them, sail by sail,

    Fierce marvels of monstrous art,

Tower darkening on tower till the sea-winds cower

crowds down as to hurl them apart.

And the windless weather is kindly,

    And comforts the host in these ;

And their hearts are uplift in them blindly,

    And blindly they boast at ease

That the next day's fight shall exalt them, and smite with

destruction the lords of the seas.

II.

And lightly the proud hearts prattle,

    And lightly the dawn draws nigh,

The dawn of the doom of the battle

    When these shall falter and fly ;

No day more great in the roll of fate filled ever with fire

the sky.

To fightward they go as to feastward,

    And the tempest of ships that drive

Sets eastward ever and eastward,

    Till closer they strain and strive ;

And the shots that rain on the hulls of Spain are as

thunders afire and alive.

And about them the blithe sea smiles

    And flashes to windward and lee

Round capes and headlands and isles

    That heed not if war there be ;

Round Sark, round Wight, green jewels of light in the

ring of the golden sea.

But the men that within them abide

    Are stout of spirit and stark

As rocks that repel the tide,

    As day that repels the dark ;

And the light bequeathed from their swords unsheathed

    shines lineal on Wight and on Sark.

And eastward the storm sets ever,

    The storm of the sails that strain

And follow and close and sever

    And lose and return and gain ;

And English thunder divides in sunder the holds of the

    ships of Spain.

Southward to Calais, appalled

    And astonished, the vast fleet veers ;

And the skies are shrouded and palled,

    But the moonless midnight hears

And sees how swift on them drive and drift strange flames

    that the darkness fears.

They fly through the night from shoreward,

    Heart-stricken till morning break,

And ever to scourge them forward

    Drives down on them England's Drake,

And hurls them in as they hurtle and spin and stagger,

    with storm to wake.

VI.

1.

And now is their time come on them. For eastward

    they drift and reel,

With the shallows of Flanders ahead, with destruction

    and havoc at heel,

With God for their comfort only, the God whom

    they serve ; and here

Their Lord, of his great loving-kindness, may revel

    and make good cheer ;

Though ever his lips wax thirstier with drinking, and
hotter the lusts in him swell ;
For he feeds the thirst that consumes him with blood,
and his winepress fumes with the reek of hell

II.

Fierce noon beats hard on the battle ; the galleons
that loom to the lee
Bow down, heel over, uplifting their shelterless hulls
from the sea :
From scuppers aspirt with blood, from guns dis-
mounted and dumb,
The signs of the doom they looked for, the loud
mute witnesses come.
They press with sunset to seaward for comfort : and
shall not they find it there ?
O servants of God most high, shall his winds not pass you
by, and his waves not spare ?

III.

The wings of the south-west wind are widened; the
breath of his fervent lips,
More keen than a sword's edge, fiercer than fire, falls full
on the plunging ships.
The pilot is he of their northward flight, their stay and
their steersman he ;
A helmsman clothed with the tempest, and girdled with
strength to constrain the sea.
And the host of them trembles and quails, caught fast in
his hand as a bird in the toils ;
For the wrath and the joy that fulfil him are mightier
than man's, whom he slays and spoils.
And vainly, with heart divided in sunder, and labour of
wavering will,
The lord of their host takes counsel with hope if haply
their star shine still,

If haply some light be left them of chance to renew and
redeem the fray ;

But the will of the black south-wester is lord of the
councils of war to-day.

One only spirit it quells not, a splendour undarkened of
chance or time ;

Be the praise of his foes with Oquendo for ever, a name
as a star sublime.

But here what aid in a hero's heart, what help in his hand
may be ?

For ever the dark wind whitens and blackens the hollows
and heights of the sea,

And galley by galley, divided and desolate, founders ; and
none takes heed,

Nor foe nor friend, if they perish ; forlorn, cast off in
their uttermost need,

They sink in the whelm of the waters, as pebbles by
children from shoreward hurled,

In the North Sea's waters that end not, nor know they a
bourn but the bourn of the world.

Past many a secure unavailable harbour, and many a loud
  stream's mouth,

Past Humber and Tees and Tyne and Tweed, they fly,
  scourged on from the south,

And torn by the scourge of the storm-wind that smites
  as a harper smites on a lyre,

And consumed of the storm as the sacrifice loved of their
  God is consumed with fire,

And devoured of the darkness as men that are slain in
  the fires of his love are devoured,

And deflowered of their lives by the storms, as by priests
  is the spirit of life deflowered.

For the wind, of its godlike mercy, relents not, and
  hounds them ahead to the north,

With English hunters at heel, till now is the herd of them
  past the Forth,

All huddled and hurtled seaward ; and now need none
  wage war upon these,

Nor huntsmen follow the quarry whose fall is the pastime
  sought of the seas.

Day upon day upon day confounds them, with measureless mists that swell,

With drift of rains everlasting and dense as the fumes of
ascending hell.

The visions of priest and of prophet beholding his
enemies bruised of his rod

Beheld but the likeness of this that is fallen on the faithful, the friends of God.

Northward, and northward, and northward they stagger
and shudder and swerve and flit,

Dismantled of masts and of yards, with sails by the fangs
of the storm-wind split.

But north of the headland whose name is Wrath, by the
wrath or the ruth of the sea,

They are swept or sustained to the westward, and drive
through the rollers aloof to the lee.

Some strive yet northward for Iceland, and perish : but
some through the storm-hewn straits

That sunder the Shetlands and Orkneys are borne of the
breath which is God's or fate's :

And some, by the dawn of September, at last give thanks
as for stars that smile,

For the winds have swept them to shelter and sight of
the cliffs of a Catholic isle.

Though many the fierce rocks feed on, and many the
merciless heretic slays,

Yet some that have laboured to land with their treasure
are trustful, and give God praise.

And the kernes of murderous Ireland, athirst with a greed
everlasting of blood,

Unslakable ever with slaughter and spoil, rage down as a
ravening flood,

To slay and to flay of their shining apparel their brethren
whom shipwreck spares ;

Such faith and such mercy, such love and such manhood,
such hands and such hearts are theirs.

Short shrift to her foes gives England, but shorter doth
Ireland to friends ; and worse

Fare they that came with a blessing on treason than they
that come with a curse.

Hacked, harried, and mangled of axes and skenes, three
   thousand naked and dead

Bear witness of Catholic Ireland, what sons of what sires
   at her breasts are bred.

Winds are pitiful, waves are merciful, tempest and storm
   are kind :

The waters that smite may spare, and the thunder is
   deaf, and the lightning is blind :

Of these perchance at his need may a man, though they
   know it not, yet find grace ;

But grace, if another be hardened against him, he gets
   not at this man's face.

For his ear that hears and his eye that sees the wreck and
   the wail of men,

And his heart that relents not within him, but hungers,
   are like as the wolf's in his den.

Worthy are these to worship their master, the murderous
   Lord of lies,

Who hath given to the pontiff his servant the keys of the
   pit and the keys of the skies.

Wild famine and red-shod rapine are cruel, and bitter
  with blood are their feasts ;

But fiercer than famine and redder than rapine the hands
  and the hearts of priests.

God, God bade these to the battle ; and here, on a land
  by his servants trod,

They perish, a lordly blood-offering, subdued by the
  hands of the servants of God.

These also were fed of his priests with faith, with the
  milk of his word and the wine ;

These too are fulfilled with the spirit of darkness that
  guided their quest divine.

And here, cast up from the ravening sea on the mild
  land's merciful breast,

This comfort they find of their fellows in worship ; this
  guerdon is theirs of their quest.

Death was captain, and doom was pilot, and darkness the
  chart of their way ;

Night and hell had in charge and in keeping the host of
  the foes of day.

Invincible, vanquished, impregnable, shattered, a sign to
  her foes of fear,

A sign to the world and the stars of laughter, the fleet of
  the Lord lies here.

Nay, for none may declare the place of the ruin wherein
  she lies ;

Nay, for none hath beholden the grave whence never a
  ghost shall rise.

The fleet of the foemen of England hath found not one
  but a thousand graves ;

And he that shall number and name them shall number
  by name and by tale the waves.

VII.

I.

Sixtus, Pope of the Church whose hope takes flight for
  heaven to dethrone the sun,

Philip, king that wouldst turn our spring to winter,
  blasted, appalled, undone,

Prince and priest, let a mourner's feast give thanks to
  God for your conquest won.

England's heel is upon you : kneel, O priest, O prince, in
the dust, and cry,

'Lord, why thus? art thou wroth with us whose faith
was great in thee, God most high?

Whence is this, that the serpent's hiss derides us? Lord,
can thy pledged word lie?

'God of hell, are its flames that swell quenched now for
ever, extinct and dead?

Who shall fear thee? or who shall hear the word thy
servants who feared thee said?

Lord, art thou as the dead gods now, whose arm is
shortened, whose rede is read?

'Yet we thought it was not for nought thy word was
given us, to guard and guide :

Yet we deemed that they had not dreamed who put their
trust in thee. Hast thou lied?

God our Lord, was the sacred sword we drew not drawn
on thy Church's side?

· England hates thee as hell's own gates ; and England

triumphs, and Rome bows down :

England mocks at thee ; England's rocks cast off thy

servants to drive and drown :

England loathes thee ; and fame betroths and plights

with England her faith for crown.

'Spain clings fast to thee ; Spain, aghast with anguish,

cries to thee ; where art thou ?

Spain puts trust in thee ; lo, the dust that soils and

darkens her prostrate brow !

Spain is true to thy service ; who shall raise up Spain for

thy service now ?

'Who shall praise thee, if none may raise thy servants

up, nor affright thy foes ?

Winter wanes, and the woods and plains forget the like-

ness of storms and snows :

So shall fear of thee fade even here : and what shall

follow thee no man knows.'

Lords of night, who would breathe your blight on April's

    morning and August's noon,

God your Lord, the condemned, the abhorred, sinks hell-

    ward, smitten with deathlike swoon :

Death's own dart in his hateful heart now thrills, and

    night shall receive him soon.

God the Devil, thy reign of revel is here for ever eclipsed

    and fled :

God the Liar, everlasting fire lays hold at last on thee,

    hand and head :

God the Accurst, the consuming thirst that burns thee

    never shall here be fed.

II.

England, queen of the waves whose green inviolate girdle

    enrings thee round,

Mother fair as the morning, where is now the place of thy

    foemen found ?

Still the sea that salutes us free proclaims them stricken,

    acclaims thee crowned.

Times may change, and the skies grow strange with signs
　　of treason and fraud and fear :
Foes in union of strange communion may rise against
　　thee from far and near :
Sloth and greed on thy strength may feed as cankers
　　waxing from year to year.

Yet, though treason and fierce unreason should league
　　and lie and defame and smite,
We that know thee, how far below thee the hatred burns
　　of the sons of night,
We that love thee, behold above thee the witness written
　　of life in light.

Life that shines from thee shows forth signs that none
　　may read not but eyeless foes :
Hate, born blind, in his abject mind grows hopeful now
　　but as madness grows :
Love, born wise, with exultant eyes adores thy glory,
　　beholds and glows.

Truth is in thee, and none may win thee to lie, forsaking
the face of truth :

Freedom lives by the grace she gives thee, born again
from thy deathless youth :

Faith should fail, and the world turn pale, wert thou the
prey of the serpent's tooth.

Greed and fraud, unabashed, unawed, may strive to sting
thee at heel in vain :

Craft and fear and mistrust may leer and mourn and
murmur and plead and plain :

Thou art thou : and thy sunbright brow is hers that
blasted the strength of Spain.

Mother, mother beloved, none other could claim in place
of thee England's place :

Earth bears none that beholds the sun so pure of record,
so clothed with grace :

Dear our mother, nor son nor brother is thine, as strong
or as fair of face.

How shalt thou be abased? or how shall fear take hold

of thy heart? of thine,

England, maiden immortal, laden with charge of life and

with hopes divine?

Earth shall wither, when eyes turned hither behold not

light in her darkness shine.

England, none that is born thy son, and lives, by grace

of thy glory, free,

Lives and yearns not at heart and burns with hope to

serve as he worships thee ;

None may sing thee : the sea-wind's wing beats down our

songs as it hails the sea.

TO A SEAMEW.

When I had wings, my brother,
  Such wings were mine as thine ;
Such life my heart remembers
In all as wild Septembers
As this when life seems other,
  Though sweet, than once was mine ;
When I had wings, my brother,
  Such wings were mine as thine.

Such life as thrills and quickens
  The silence of thy flight,
Or fills thy note's elation
With lordlier exultation

Than man's, whose faint heart sickens
  With hopes and fears that blight
Such life as thrills and quickens
  The silence of thy flight.

Thy cry from windward clanging
  Makes all the cliffs rejoice;
Though storm clothe seas with sorrow,
Thy call salutes the morrow;
While shades of pain seem hanging
  Round earth's most rapturous voice,
Thy cry from windward clanging
  Makes all the cliffs rejoice.

We, sons and sires of seamen,
  Whose home is all the sea,
What place man may, we claim it;
But thine—whose thought may name it?

TO A SEAMEW.

Free birds live higher than freemen,
  And gladlier ye than we—
We, sons and sires of seamen,
  Whose home is all the sea.

For you the storm sounds only
  More notes of more delight
Than earth's in sunniest weather:
When heaven and sea together
Join strengths against the lonely
  Lost bark borne down by night,
For you the storm sounds only
  More notes of more delight.

With wider wing, and louder
  Long clarion-call of joy,
Thy tribe salutes the terror
Of darkness, wild as error,

But sure as truth, and prouder

   Than waves with man for toy;

With wider wing, and louder

   Long clarion-call of joy.

The wave's wing spreads and flutters,

   The wave's heart swells and breaks;

One moment's passion thrills it,

One pulse of power fulfils it

And ends the pride it utters

   When, loud with life that quakes,

The wave's wing spreads and flutters,

   The wave's heart swells and breaks.

But thine and thou, my brother,

   Keep heart and wing more high

Than aught may scare or sunder;

The waves whose throats are thunder

Fall hurtling each on other,
  And triumph as they die ;
But thine and thou, my brother,
  Keep heart and wing more high.

More high than wrath or anguish,
  More strong than pride or fear,
The sense or soul half hidden
In thee, for us forbidden,
Bids thee nor change nor languish,
  But live thy life as here,
More high than wrath or anguish,
  More strong than pride or fear.

We are fallen, even we, whose passion
  On earth is nearest thine ;
Who sing, and cease from flying ;
Who live, and dream of dying :

TO A SEAMEW.

Grey time, in time's grey fashion,
  Bids wingless creatures pine :
We are fallen, even we, whose passion
  On earth is nearest thine.

The lark knows no such rapture,
  Such joy no nightingale,
As sways the songless measure
Wherein thy wings take pleasure :
Thy love may no man capture,
  Thy pride may no man quail ;
The lark knows no such rapture,
  Such joy no nightingale.

And we, whom dreams embolden,
  We can but creep and sing
And watch through heaven's waste hollow
The flight no sight may follow

To the utter bourne beholden

Of none that lack thy wing :

And we, whom dreams embolden,

We can but creep and sing.

Our dreams have wings that falter,

Our hearts bear hopes that die ;

For thee no dream could better

A life no fears may fetter,

A pride no care can alter,

That wots not whence or why

Our dreams have wings that falter,

Our hearts bear hopes that die.

With joy more fierce and sweeter

Than joys we deem divine

Their lives, by time untarnished,

Are girt about and garnished,

Who match the wave's full metre

   And drink the wind's wild wine

With joy more fierce and sweeter

   Than joys we deem divine.

Ah, well were I for ever,

   Wouldst thou change lives with me,

And take my song's wild honey,

And give me back thy sunny

Wide eyes that weary never,

   And wings that search the sea ;

Ah, well were I for ever,

   Wouldst thou change lives with me.

Beachy Head, September, 1886.

PAN AND THALASSIUS.

A LYRICAL IDYL.

THALASSIUS.

PAN !

PAN.

O sea-stray, seed of Apollo,

What word wouldst thou have with me?

My ways thou wast fain to follow

Or ever the years hailed thee

Man.

Now

If August brood on the valleys,

If satyrs laugh on the lawns,

What part in the wildwood alleys

Hast thou with the fleet-foot fauns—

Thou ?

See !

Thy feet are a man's—not cloven

 Like these, not light as a boy's :

The tresses and tendrils inwoven

 That lure us, the lure of them cloys

  Thee.

  Us

The joy of the wild woods never

 Leaves free of the thirst it slakes :

The wild love throbs in us ever

 That burns in the dense hot brakes

  Thus.

  Life,

Eternal, passionate, awless,

 Insatiable, mutable, dear,

Makes all men's law for us lawless :

 We strive not : how should we fear

  Strife ?

˄   We,

The birds and the bright winds know not

Such joys as are ours in the mild

Warm woodland; joys such as grow not

In waste green fields of the wild

Sea.

No;

Long since, in the world's wind veering,

Thy heart was estranged from me :

Sweet Echo shall yield thee not hearing :

What have we to do with thee?

Go.

THALASSIUS.

Ay !

Such wrath on thy nostril quivers

As once in Sicilian heat

Bade herdsmen quail, and the rivers

Shrank, leaving a path for thy feet

Dry?

Nay,

Low down in the hot soft hollow

Too snakelike hisses thy spleen :

‘O sea-stray, seed of Apollo !’

What ill hast thou heard or seen ?

Say.

Man

Knows well, if he hears beside him

The snarl of thy wrath at noon,

What evil may soon betide him,

Or late, if thou smite not soon,

Pan.

Me

The sound of thy flute, that flatters

The woods as they smile and sigh,

Charmed fast as it charms thy satyrs,

Can charm no faster than I

Thee.

Fast

Thy music may charm the splendid

Wide woodland silence to sleep

With sounds and dreams of thee blended

And whispers of waters that creep

Past.

Here

The spell of thee breathes and passes

And bids the heart in me pause,

Hushed soft as the leaves and the grasses

Are hushed if the storm's foot draws

Near.

Yet

The panic that strikes down strangers

Transgressing thy ways unaware

Affrights not me nor endangers

Through dread of thy secret snare

Set.

PAN.

Whence

May man find heart to deride me?

Who made his face as a star

To shine as a God's beside me?

Nay, get thee away from us, far

Hence.

THALASSIUS.

Then

Shall no man's heart, as he raises

A hymn to thy secret head,

Wax great with the godhead he praises :

Thou, God, shalt be like unto dead

Men.

PAN.

Grace

I take not of men's thanksgiving,

I crave not of lips that live ;

They die, and behold, I am living,

While they and their dead Gods give

Place.

THALASSIUS.

Yea:

Too lightly the words were spoken

That mourned or mocked at thee dead:

But whose was the word, the token,

The song that answered and said

Nay?

PAN.

Whose

But mine, in the midnight hidden,

Clothed round with the strength of night

And mysteries of things forbidden

For all but the one most bright

Muse?

PAN AND THALASSIUS.

Hers

Or thine, O Pan, was the token

That gave back empire to thee

When power in thy hands lay broken

As reeds that quake if a bee

Stirs?

Whom

Have I in my wide woods need of?

Urania's limitless eyes

Behold not mine end, though they read of

A word that shall speak to the skies

Doom.

She

Gave back to thee kingdom and glory,

And grace that was thine of yore,

And life to thy leaves, late hoary

   As weeds cast up from the hoar

      Sea.

      Song

Can bid faith shine as the morning

   Though light in the world be none :

Death shrinks if her tongue sound warning,

   Night quails, and beholds the sun

      Strong.

PAN.

   Night

Bare rule over men for ages

   Whose worship wist not of me

And gat but sorrows for wages,

   And hardly for tears could see

      Light.

      Call

No more on the starry presence

   Whose light through the long dark swam :

Hold fast to the green world's pleasance:

For I that am lord of it am

All.

THALASSIUS.

God,

God Pan, from the glad wood's portal

The breaths of thy song blow sweet:

But woods may be walked in of mortal

Man's thought, where never thy feet

Trod.

Thine

All secrets of growth and of birth are,

All glories of flower and of tree,

Wheresoever the wonders of earth are;

The words of the spell of the sea

Mine.

A BALLAD OF BATH.

LIKE a queen enchanted who may not laugh or weep,

    Glad at heart and guarded from change and care like

    ours,

Girt about with beauty by days and nights that creep

Soft as breathless ripples that softly shoreward sweep,

    Lies the lovely city whose grace no grief deflowers.

Age and grey forgetfulness, time that shifts and veers,

Touch not thee, our fairest, whose charm no rival

    nears,

    Hailed as England's Florence of one whose praise gives

    grace,

Landor, once thy lover, a name that love reveres:

    Dawn and noon and sunset are one before thy face.

Dawn whereof we know not, and noon whose fruit we
  reap,
  Garnered up in record of years that fell like flowers,
Sunset liker sunrise along the shining steep
Whence thy fair face lightens, and where thy soft springs
  leap,
  Crown at once and gird thee with grace of guardian
  powers.
Loved of men beloved of us, souls that fame inspheres,
All thine air hath music for him who dreams and hears ;
  Voices mixed of multitudes, feet of friends that pace,
Witness why for ever, if heaven's face clouds or clears,
  Dawn and noon and sunset are one before thy face.

Peace hath here found harbourage mild as very sleep :
  Not the hills and waters, the fields and wildwood
  bowers,
Smile or speak more tenderly, clothed with peace more
  deep,
Here than memory whispers of days our memories keep

Fast with love and laughter and dreams of withered

   hours.

Bright were these as blossom of old, and thought endears

Still the fair soft phantoms that pass with smiles or tears,

   Sweet as roseleaves hoarded and dried wherein we trace

Still the soul and spirit of sense that lives and cheers :

   Dawn and noon and sunset are one before thy face.

City lulled asleep by the chime of passing years,

Sweeter smiles thy rest than the radiance round thy peers;

   Only love and lovely remembrance here have place.

Time on thee lies lighter than music on men's ears ;

   Dawn and noon and sunset are one before thy face.

IN A GARDEN.

BABY, see the flowers !

—Baby sees

Fairer things than these,

Fairer though they be than dreams of ours.

Baby, hear the birds !

—Baby knows

Better songs than those,

Sweeter though they sound than sweetest words.

Baby, see the moon !

—Baby's eyes

Laugh to watch it rise,

Answering light with love and night with noon.

Baby, hear the sea !

—Baby's face

Takes a graver grace,

Touched with wonder what the sound may be.

Baby, see the star !

—Baby's hand

Opens, warm and bland,

Calm in claim of all things fair that are.

Baby, hear the bells !

—Baby's head

Bows, as ripe for bed,

Now the flowers curl round and close their cells.

Baby, flower of light,

Sleep, and see

Brighter dreams than we,

Till good day shall smile away good night.

A RHYME.

Babe, if rhyme be none
  For that sweet small word
Babe, the sweetest one
  Ever heard,

Right it is and meet
  Rhyme should keep not true
Time with such a sweet
  Thing as you.

Meet it is that rhyme
  Should not gain such grace:
What is April's prime
  To your face?

What to yours is May's
  Rosiest smile? what sound
Like your laughter sways
  All hearts round?

None can tell in metre
  Fit for ears on earth
What sweet star grew sweeter
  At your birth.

Wisdom doubts what may be :
  Hope, with smile sublime,
Trusts : but neither, baby,
  Knows the rhyme.

Wisdom lies down lonely ;
  Hope keeps watch from far ;
None but one seer only
  Sees the star.

Love alone, with yearning

   Heart for astrolabe,

Takes the star's height, burning

   O'er the babe.

BABY-BIRD.

BABY-BIRD, baby-bird,
    Ne'er a song on earth
May be heard, may be heard,
    Rich as yours in mirth.

All your flickering fingers,
    All your twinkling toes,
Play like light that lingers
    Till the clear song close.

Baby-bird, baby-bird,
    Your grave majestic eyes
Like a bird's warbled words
    Speak, and sorrow dies.

Sorrow dies for love's sake,
   Love grows one with mirth,
Even for one white dove's sake,
   Born a babe on earth.

Baby-bird, baby-bird,
   Chirping loud and long,
Other birds hush their words,
   Hearkening toward your song.

Sweet as spring though it ring,
   Full of love's own lures,
Weak and wrong sounds their song,
   Singing after yours.

Baby-bird, baby-bird,
   The happy heart that hears
Seems to win back within
   Heaven, and cast out fears.

BABY-BIRD.

Earth and sun seem as one
  Sweet light and one sweet word
Known of none here but one,
  Known of one sweet bird.

OLIVE.

I.

WHO may praise her?
Eyes where midnight shames the sun,
Hair of night and sunshine spun,
Woven of dawn's or twilight's loom,
Radiant darkness, lustrous gloom,
Godlike childhood's flowerlike bloom,
None may praise aright, nor sing
Half the grace wherewith like spring
Love arrays her.

II.

Love untold
Sings in silence, speaks in light
Shed from each fair feature, bright

Still from heaven, whence toward us, now

Nine years since, she deigned to bow

Down the brightness of her brow,

Deigned to pass through mortal birth :

Reverence calls her, here on earth,

　　Nine years old.

III.

Love's deep duty,

Even when love transfigured grows

Worship, all too surely knows

How, though love may cast out fear,

Yet the debt divine and dear

Due to childhood's godhead here

May by love of man be paid

Never ; never song be made

　　Worth its beauty.

IV.

Nought is all
Sung or said or dreamed or thought
Ever, set beside it ; nought
All the love that man may give—
Love whose prayer should be, ' Forgive !'
Heaven, we see, on earth may live ;
Earth can thank not heaven, we know,
Save with songs that ebb and flow,
 Rise and fall.

V.

No man living,
No man dead, save haply one
Now gone homeward past the sun,
Ever found such grace as might
Tune his tongue to praise aright
Children, flowers of love and light,

Whom our praise dispraises : we

Sing, in sooth, but not as he

    Sang thanksgiving.

VI.

    Hope that smiled,

Seeing her new-born beauty, made

Out of heaven's own light and shade,

Smiled not half so sweetly : love,

Seeing the sun, afar above,

Warm the nest that rears the dove,

Sees, more bright than moon or sun,

All the heaven of heavens in one

    Little child.

VII.

    Who may sing her ?

Wings of angels when they stir

Make no music worthy her :

Sweeter sound her shy soft words

Here than songs of God's own birds

Whom the fire of rapture girds

Round with light from love's face lit :

Hands of angels find no fit

    Gifts to bring her.

VIII.

    Babes at birth

Wear as raiment round them cast,

Keep as witness toward their past,

Tokens left of heaven ; and each,

Ere its lips learn mortal speech,

Ere sweet heaven pass on pass reach,

Bears in undiverted eyes

Proof of unforgotten skies

    Here on earth.

IX.

Quenched as embers

Quenched with flakes of rain or snow

Till the last faint flame burns low,

All those lustrous memories lie

Dead with babyhood gone by :

Yet in her they dare not die :

Others, fair as heaven is, yet,

Now they share not heaven, forget :

She remembers.

A WORD WITH THE WIND.

LORD of days and nights that hear thy word of wintry
 warning,
Wind, whose feet are set on ways that none may tread,
Change the nest wherein thy wings are fledged for flight
 by morning,
 Change the harbour whence at dawn thy sails are spread.
Not the dawn, ere yet the imprisoning night has half
 released her,
 More desires the sun's full face of cheer, than we,
Well as yet we love the strength of the iron-tongued
 north-easter,
 Yearn for wind to meet us as we front the sea.
All thy ways are good, O wind, and all the world should
 fester,
 Were thy fourfold godhead quenched, or stilled thy
 strife :

III.   H

Yet the waves and we desire too long the deep south·
    wester,

  Whence the waters quicken shoreward, clothed with
    life.

Yet the field not made for ploughing save of keels nor
    harrowing

  Save of storm-winds lies unbrightened by thy breath :

Banded broad with ruddy samphire glow the sea-banks
    narrowing

  Westward, while the sea gleams chill and still as
    death.

Sharp and strange from inland sounds thy bitter note of
    battle,

  Blown between grim skies and waters sullen-souled,

Till the baffled seas bear back, rocks roar and shingles
    rattle,

  Vexed and angered and anhungered and acold.

Change thy note, and give the waves their will, and all
    the measure,

  Full and perfect, of the music of their might,

Let it fill the bays with thunderous notes and throbs of

    pleasure,

  Shake the shores with passion, sound at once and

    smite.

Sweet are even the mild low notes of wind and sea, but

    sweeter

  Sounds the song whose choral wrath of raging rhyme

Bids the shelving shoals keep tune with storm's imperious

    metre,

  Bids the rocks and reefs respond in rapturous chime.

Sweet the lisp and lulling whisper and luxurious laughter,

  Soft as love or sleep, of waves whereon the sun

Dreams, and dreams not of the darkling hours before nor

    after,

  Winged with cloud whose wrath shall bid love's day be

    done.

Yet shall darkness bring the awakening sea a lordlier

    lover,

  Clothed with strength more amorous and more

    strenuous will,

Whence her heart of hearts shall kindle and her soul
    recover

  Sense of love too keen to lie for love's sake still.

Let thy strong south-western music sound, and bid the
    billows

    Brighten, proud and glad to feel thy scourge and
      kiss

Sting and soothe and sway them, bowed as aspens bend
    or willows,

    Yet resurgent still in breathless rage of bliss.

All to-day the slow sleek ripples hardly bear up shore-
    ward,

    Charged with sighs more light than laughter, faint and
      fair,

Like a woodland lake's weak wavelets lightly lingering
    forward,

    Soft and listless as the slumber-stricken air.

Be the sunshine bared or veiled, the sky superb or
    shrouded,

    Still the waters, lax and languid, chafed and foiled,

Keen and thwarted, pale and patient, clothed with fire or
   clouded,
   Vex their heart in vain, or sleep like serpents coiled.
Thee they look for, blind and baffled, wan with wrath and
   weary,
   Blown for ever back by winds that rock the bird:
Winds that seamews breast subdue the sea, and bid the
   dreary
   Waves be weak as hearts made sick with hope de-
   ferred.
Let thy clarion sound from westward, let the south bear
   token
   How the glories of thy godhead sound and shine:
Bid the land rejoice to see the land-wind's broad wings
   broken,   .
   Bid the sea take comfort, bid the world be thine.
Half the world abhors thee beating back the sea, and
   blackening
   Heaven with fierce and woful change of fluctuant
   form:

All the world acclaims thee shifting sail again, and slack-
ening

Cloud by cloud the close-reefed cordage of the storm.

Sweeter fields and brighter woods and lordlier hills than
waken

Here at sunrise never hailed the sun and thee :

Turn thee then, and give them comfort, shed like rain
and shaken

Far as foam that laughs and leaps along the sea.

FAR off is the sea, and the land is afar :

  The low banks reach at the sky,

  Seen hence, and are heavenward high ;

Though light for the leap of a boy they are,

  And the far sea late was nigh.

The fair wild fields and the circling downs,

  The bright sweet marshes and meads

  All glorious with flowerlike weeds,

The great grey churches, the sea-washed towns,

  Recede as a dream recedes.

The world draws back, and the world's light wanes,

  As a dream dies down and is dead ;

  And the clouds and the gleams overhead

Change, and change ; and the sea remains,

    A shadow of dreamlike dread.

Wild, and woful, and pale, and grey,

    A shadow of sleepless fear,

    A corpse with the night for bier,

The fairest thing that beholds the day

    Lies haggard and hopeless here.

And the wind's wings, broken and spent, subside ;

    And the dumb waste world is hoar,

    And strange as the sea the shore ;

And shadows of shapeless dreams abide

    Where life may abide no more.

A sail to seaward, a sound from shoreward,

    And the spell were broken that seems

    To reign in a world of dreams

Where vainly the dreamer's feet make forward

    And vainly the low sky gleams.

The sea-forsaken forlorn deep-wrinkled

    Salt slanting stretches of sand

    That slope to the seaward hand,

Were they fain of the ripples that flashed and

    twinkled

    And laughed as they struck the strand?

As bells on the reins of the fairies ring

    The ripples that kissed them rang,

    The light from the sundawn sprang,

And the sweetest of songs that the world may sing

    Was theirs when the full sea sang.

Now no light is in heaven ; and now

    Not a note of the sea-wind's tune

    Rings hither : the bleak sky's boon

Grants hardly sight of a grey sun's brow—

    A sun more sad than the moon.

More sad than a moon that clouds beleaguer

And storm is a scourge to smite,

The sick sun's shadowlike light

Grows faint as the clouds and the waves wax eager,

And withers away from sight.

The day's heart cowers, and the night's heart

    quickens:

Full fain would the day be dead

And the stark night reign in his stead :

The sea falls dumb as the sea-fog thickens

And the sunset dies for dread.

Outside of the range of time, whose breath

Is keen as the manslayer's knife

And his peace but a truce for strife,

Who knows if haply the shadow of death

May be not the light of life?

For the storm and the rain and the darkness borrow

    But an hour from the suns to be,

    But a strange swift passage, that we

May rejoice, who have mourned not to-day, to-morrow,

    In the sun and the wind and the sea.

BY THE WAYSIDE.

SUMMER'S face was rosiest, skies and woods were mellow,
Earth had heaven to friend, and heaven had earth to
 fellow,
 When we met where wooded hills and meadows
 meet.
Autumn's face is pale, and all her late leaves yellow,
 Now that here again we greet.

Wan with years whereof this eightieth nears December,
 Fair and bright with love, the kind old face I know
Shines above the sweet small twain whose eyes remember
Heaven, and fill with April's light this pale November,
 Though the dark year's glass run low.

Like a rose whose joy of life her silence utters

When the birds are loud, and low the lulled wind
   mutters,
   Grave and silent shines the boy nigh three years old.

Wise and sweet his smile, that falters not nor flutters,
   Glows, and turns the gloom to gold.

Like the new-born sun's that strikes the dark and slays it,
   So that even for love of light it smiles and dies,
Laughs the boy's blithe face whose fair fourth year
   arrays it
All with light of life and mirth that stirs and sways it
   And fulfils the deep wide eyes.

Wide and warm with glowing laughter's exultation,
Full of welcome, full of sunbright jubilation,
   Flash my taller friend's quick eyebeams, charged with
   glee ;
But with softer still and sweeter salutation
   Shine my smaller friend's on me.

Little arms flung round my bending neck, that yoke it
  Fast in tender bondage, draw my face down too
Toward the flower-soft face whose dumb deep smiles
    invoke it ,
Dumb, but love can read the radiant eyes that woke it,
  Blue as June's mid heaven is blue.

How may men find refuge, how should hearts be
    shielded,
From the weapons thus by little children wielded,
    When they lift such eyes as light this lustrous face—
Eyes that woke love sleeping unawares, and yielded
  Love for love, a gift of grace,

Grace beyond man's merit, love that laughs, forgiving
  Even the sin of being no more a child, nor worth
Trust and love that lavish gifts above man's giving,
Touch or glance of eyes and lips the sweetest living,
  Fair as heaven and kind as earth ?

NIGHT.

I.

FROM THE ITALIAN OF GIOVANNI STROZZI.

NIGHT, whom in shape so sweet thou here may'st see
  Sleeping, was by an Angel sculptured thus
  In marble, and since she sleeps hath life like us :
Thou doubt'st? Awake her : she will speak to thee.

II.

FROM THE ITALIAN OF MICHELANGELO BUONARROTI.

Sleep likes me well, and better yet to know
  I am but stone.   While shame and grief must be,
  Good hap is mine, to feel not, nor to see :
Take heed, then, lest thou wake me : ah, speak low.

IN TIME OF MOURNING.

'RETURN,' we dare not as we fain

    Would cry from hearts that yearn :

Love dares not bid our dead again

    Return.

    O hearts that strain and burn

As fires fast fettered burn and strain !

    Bow down, lie still, and learn.

The heart that healed all hearts of pain

    No funeral rites inurn :

Its echoes, while the stars remain,

    Return.

May, 1885.

THE INTERPRETERS.

I.

Days dawn on us that make amends for many
    Sometimes,
When heaven and earth seem sweeter even than any
    Man's rhymes.

Light had not all been quenched in France, or quelled
    In Greece,
Had Homer sung not, or had Hugo held
    His peace.

Had Sappho's self not left her word thus long
    For token,
The sea round Lesbos yet in waves of song
    Had spoken.

III.

II.

And yet these days of subtler air and finer
> Delight,
When lovelier looks the darkness, and diviner
> The light—

The gift they give of all these golden hours,
> Whose urn
Pours forth reverberate rays or shadowing showers
> In turn—

Clouds, beams, and winds that make the live day's track
> Seem living—
What were they did no spirit give them back
> Thanksgiving?

III.

Dead air, dead fire, dead shapes and shadows, telling
> Time nought ;
Man gives them sense and soul by song, and dwelling
> In thought.

In human thought their being endures, their power

    Abides :

Else were their life a thing that each light hour

    Derides.

The years live, work, sigh, smile, and die, with all

    They cherish ;

The soul endures, though dreams that fed it fall

    And perish.

IV.

In human thought have all things habitation ;

    Our days

Laugh, lower, and lighten past, and find no station

    That stays.

But thought and faith are mightier things than time

    Can wrong,

Made splendid once with speech, or made sublime

    By song.

Remembrance, though the tide of change that rolls

    Wax hoary,

Gives earth and heaven, for song's sake and the soul's,

    Their glory.

    July 16th, 1885.

THE RECALL.

RETURN, they cry, ere yet your day
  Set, and the sky grow stern :
Return, strayed souls, while yet ye may
  Return.

But heavens beyond us yearn ;
Yea, heights of heaven above the sway
  Of stars that eyes discern.

The soul whose wings from shoreward stray
  Makes toward her viewless bourne
Though trustless faith and unfaith say,
  Return.

BY TWILIGHT.

IF we dream that desire of the distance above us
Should be fettered by fear of the shadows that seem,
If we wake, to be nought, but to hate or to love us
If we dream,

Night sinks on the soul, and the stars as they gleam
Speak menace or mourning, with tongues to reprove us
That we deemed of them better than terror may deem.

But if hope may not lure us, if fear may not move us,
Thought lightens the darkness wherein the supreme
Pure presence of death shall assure us, and prove us
If we dream.

A BABY'S EPITAPH.

APRIL made me : winter laid me here away asleep.

Bright as Maytime was my daytime ; night is soft and
deep :

Though the morrow bring forth sorrow, well are ye that
weep.

Ye that held me dear beheld me not a twelvemonth
long :

All the while ye saw me smile, ye knew not whence the
song

Came that made me smile, and laid me here, and wrought
you wrong.

Angels, calling from your brawling world one undefiled,

Homeward bade me, and forbade me here to rest beguiled :

Here I sleep not : pass, and weep not here upon your
child.

ON THE DEATH OF SIR HENRY TAYLOR.

FOURSCORE and five times has the gradual year

  Risen and fulfilled its days of youth and eld

  Since first the child's eyes opening first beheld

Light, who now leaves-behind to help us here

Light shed from song as starlight from a sphere

  Serene as summer ; song whose charm compelled

  The sovereign soul made flesh in Artevelde

To stand august before us and austere,

Half sad with mortal knowledge, all sublime

With trust that takes no taint from change or time,

Trust in man's might of manhood.   Strong and sage,

  Clothed round with reverence of remembering hearts,

He, twin-born with our nigh departing age,

  Into the light of peace and fame departs.

IN MEMORY OF JOHN WILLIAM INCHBOLD.

FAREWELL : how should not such as thou fare well,

   Though we fare ill that love thee, and that live,

And know, whate'er the days wherein we dwell

   May give us, thee again they will not give?

Peace, rest, and sleep are all we know of death,

   And all we dream of comfort : yet for thee,

Whose breath of life was bright and strenuous breath,

   We think the change is other than we see.

The seal of sleep set on thine eyes to-day

   Surely can seal not up the keen swift light

That lit them once for ever.   Night can slay

   None save the children of the womb of night.

The fire that burns up dawn to bring forth noon

    Was father of thy spirit : how shouldst thou

Die as they die for whom the sun and moon

    Are silent?   Thee the darkness holds not now :

Them, while they looked upon the light, and deemed

    That life was theirs for living in the sun,

The darkness held in bondage : and they dreamed,

    Who knew not that such life as theirs was none.

To thee the sun spake, and the morning sang

    Notes deep and clear as life or heaven : the sea

That sounds for them but wild waste music rang

    Notes that were lost not when they rang for thee.

The mountains clothed with light and night and change.

    The lakes alive with wind and cloud and sun

Made answer, by constraint sublime and strange,

    To the ardent hand that bade thy will be done.

We may not bid the mountains mourn, the sea

   That lived and lightened from thine hand again

Moan, as of old would men that mourned as we

   A man beloved, a man elect of men,

A man that loved them.   Vain, divine and vain,

   The dream that touched with thoughts or tears of ours

The spirit of sense that lives in sun and rain,

   Sings out in birds, and breathes and fades in flowers.

Not for our joy they live, and for our grief

   They die not.   Though thine eye be closed, thine hand

Powerless as mine to paint them, not a leaf

   In English woods or glades of Switzerland

Falls earlier now, fades faster.   All our love

   Moves not our mother's changeless heart, who gives

A little light to eyes and stars above,

   A little life to each man's heart that lives.

A little life to heaven and earth and sea,

    To stars and souls revealed of night and day,

And change, the one thing changeless : yet shall she

    Cease too, perchance, and perish.   Who shall say ?

Our mother Nature, dark and sweet as sleep,

    And strange as life and strong as death, holds fast,

Even as she holds our hearts alive, the deep

    Dumb secret of her first-born births and last.

But this, we know, shall cease not till the strife

    Of nights and days and fears and hopes find end ;

This, through the brief eternities of life,

    Endures, and calls from death a living friend ;

The love made strong with knowledge, whence confirmed

    The whole soul takes assurance, and the past

(So by time's measure, not by memory's, termed)

    Lives present life, and mingles first with last.

I, now long since thy guest of many days,

    Who found thy hearth a brother's, and with thee

Tracked in and out the lines of rolling bays

    And banks and gulfs and reaches of the sea—

Deep dens wherein the wrestling water sobs

    And pants with restless pain of refluent breath

Till all the sunless hollow sounds and throbs

    With ebb and flow of eddies dark as death—

I know not what more glorious world, what waves

    More bright with life,—if brighter aught may live

Than those that filled and fled their tidal caves—

    May now give back the love thou hast to give.

Tintagel, and the long Trebarwith sand,

    Lone Camelford, and Boscastle divine

With dower of southern blossom, bright and bland

    Above the roar of granite-baffled brine,

Shall hear no more by joyous night or day

    From downs or causeways good to rove and ride

Or feet of ours or horse-hoofs urge their way

    That sped us here and there by tower and tide.

The headlands and the hollows and the waves,

    For all our love, forget us : where I am

Thou art not : deeper sleeps the shadow on graves

    Than in the sunless gulf that once we swam.

Thou hast swum too soon the sea of death : for us

    Too soon, but if truth bless love's blind belief

Faith, born of hope and memory, says not thus :

    And joy for thee for me should mean not grief.

And joy for thee, if ever soul of man

    Found joy in change and life of ampler birth

Than here pens in the spirit for a span,

    Must be the life that doubt calls death on earth.

For if, beyond the shadow and the sleep,

    A place there be for souls without a stain,

Where peace is perfect, and delight more deep

    Than seas or skies that change and shine again,

There none of all unsullied souls that live

    May hold a surer station : none may lend

More light to hope's or memory's lamp, nor give

    More joy than thine to those that called thee friend.

Yea, joy from sorrow's barren womb is born

    When faith begets on grief the godlike child .

As midnight yearns with starry sense of morn

    In Arctic summers, though the sea wax wild,

So love, whose name is memory, thrills at heart,

    Remembering and rejoicing in thee, now

Alive where love may dream not what thou art

    But knows that higher than hope or love art thou.

' Whatever heaven, if heaven at all may be,

   Await the sacred souls of good men dead,

There, now we mourn who loved him here, is he.'

   So, sweet and stern of speech, the Roman said,

Erect in grief, in trust erect, and gave

   His deathless dead a deathless life even here

Where day bears down on day as wave on wave

   And not man's smile fades faster than his tear

Albeit this gift be given not me to give,

   Nor power be mine to break time's silent spell,

Not less shall love that dies not while I live

   Bid thee, beloved in life and death, farewell.

NEW YEARS DAY.

New Year, be good to England. Bid her name
Shine sunlike as of old on all the sea :
Make strong her soul : set all her spirit free :
Bind fast her homeborn foes with links of shame
More strong than iron and more keen than flame :
    Seal up their lips for shame's sake : so shall she
    Whc was the light that lightened freedom be,
For all false tongues, in all men's eyes the same.

O last-born child of Time, earth's eldest lord,
    God undiscrowned of godhead, who for man
        Begets all good and evil things that live,
Do thou, his new-begotten son, implored
    Of hearts that hope and fear not, make thy span
        Bright with such light as history bids thee give.

Jan. 1, 1889.

TO SIR RICHARD F. BURTON.

(ON HIS TRANSLATION OF THE ARABIAN NIGHTS.)

WESTWARD the sun sinks, grave and glad ; but far
    Eastward, with laughter and tempestuous tears,
    Cloud, rain, and splendour as of orient spears,
Keen as the sea's thrill toward a kindling star,
The sundawn breaks the barren twilight's bar
      And fires the mist and slays it.   Years on years
      Vanish, but he that hearkens eastward hears
Bright music from the world where shadows are.

Where shadows are not shadows.   Hand in hand
A man's word bids them rise and smile and stand
      And triumph.   All that glorious orient glows
Defiant of the dusk.   Our twilight land
      Trembles ; but all the heaven is all one rose,
      Whence laughing love dissolves her frosts and snows.

NELL GWYN.

Sweet heart, that no taint of the throne or the stage

Could touch with unclean transformation, or alter

To the likeness of courtiers whose consciences falter

At the smile or the frown, at the mirth or the rage,

Of a master whom chance could inflame or assuage,

Our Lady of Laughter, invoked in no psalter,

Adored of no faithful that cringe and that palter,

Praise be with thee yet from a hag-ridden age.

Our Lady of Pity thou wast : and to thee

All England, whose sons are the sons of the sea,

Gives thanks, and will hear not if history snarls

When the name of the friend of her sailors is spoken :

And thy lover she cannot but love—by the token

That thy name was the last on the lips of King Charles.

CALIBAN ON ARIEL

'His backward voice is to utter foul speeches and to detract.'

THE tongue is loosed of that most lying slave,

    Whom stripes may move, not kindness.   Listen : 'Lo,

    The real god of song, Lord Stephano,

That's a brave god, if ever god were brave,

And bears celestial liquor : but,' the knave

    (A most ridiculous monster) howls, 'we know

    From Ariel's lips what springs of poison flow,

The chicken-heart blasphemer !   Hear him rave !'

Thou poisonous slave, got by the devil himself

    Upon thy wicked dam, the witch whose name

      Is darkness, and the sun her eyes' offence,

Though hell's hot sewerage breed no loathlier elf,

    Men cry not shame upon thee, seeing thy shame

      So perfect : they but bid thee—'Hag-seed, hence !'

THE WEARY WEDDING.

O DAUGHTER, why do ye laugh and weep,
    One with another?
For woe to wake and for will to sleep,
    Mother, my mother.

But weep ye winna the day ye wed,
    One with another.
For tears are dry when the springs are dead,
    Mother, my mother.

Too long have your tears run down like rain,
    One with another.
For a long love lost and a sweet love slain,
    Mother, my mother.

Too long have your tears dripped down like dew,

    One with another.

For a knight that my sire and my brethren slew,

    Mother, my mother.

Let past things perish and dead griefs lie,

    One with another.

O fain would I weep not, and fain would I die,

    Mother, my mother.

Fair gifts we give ye, to laugh and live,

    One with another.

But sair and strange are the gifts I give,

    Mother, my mother.

And what will ye give for your father's love ?

    One with another.

Fruits full few and thorns enough,

    Mother, my mother.

And what will ye give for your mother's sake ?

One with another.

Tears to brew and tares to bake,

Mother, my mother.

And what will ye give your sister Jean ?

One with another.

A bier to build and a babe to wean,

Mother, my mother.

And what will ye give your sister Nell ?

One with another.

The end of life and beginning of hell,

Mother, my mother.

And what will ye give your sister Kate ?

One with another.

Earth's door and hell's gate,

Mother, my mother.

And what will ye give your brother Will?

   One with another.

Life's grief and world's ill,

   Mother, my mother.

And what will ye give your brother Hugh?

   One with another.

A bed of turf to turn into,

   Mother, my mother.

And what will ye give your brother John?

   One with another.

The dust of death to feed upon,

   Mother, my mother.

And what will ye give your bauld bridegroom?

   One with another.

A barren bed and an empty room,

   Mother, my mother.

And what will ye give your bridegroom's friend?

 One with another.

A weary foot to the weary end,

 Mother, my mother.

And what will ye give your blithe bridesmaid?

 One with another.

Grief to sew and sorrow to braid,

 Mother, my mother.

And what will ye drink the day ye're wed?

 One with another.

But ae drink of the wan well-head,

 Mother, my mother.

And whatten a water is that to draw?

 One with another.

We maun draw thereof a', we maun drink thereof a',

 Mother, my mother.

And what shall ye pu' where the well rins deep?

> One with another.

Green herb of death, fine flower of sleep,

> Mother, my mother.

Are there ony fishes that swim therein?

> One with another.

The white fish grace, and the red fish sin,

> Mother, my mother.

Are there ony birds that sing thereby?

> One with another.

O when they come thither they sing till they die,

> Mother, my mother.

Is there ony draw-bucket to that well-head?

> One with another.

There's a wee well-bucket hangs low by a thread,

> Mother, my mother.

And whatten a thread is that to spin?

One with another.

It's green for grace, and it's black for sin,

Mother, my mother.

And what will ye strew on your bride-chamber floor?

One with another.

But one strewing and no more,

Mother, my mother.

And whatten a strewing shall that one be?

One with another.

The dust of earth and sand of the sea,

Mother, my mother.

And what will ye take to build your bed?

One with another.

Sighing and shame and the bones of the dead,

Mother, my mother.

And what will ye wear for your wedding gown ?

   One with another.

Grass for the green and dust for the brown,

   Mother, my mother.

And what will ye wear for your wedding lace ?

   One with another.

A heavy heart and a hidden face,

   Mother, my mother.

And what will ye wear for a wreath to your head ?

   One with another.

Ash for the white and blood for the red,

   Mother, my mother.

And what will ye wear for your wedding ring ?

   One with another.

A weary thought for a weary thing,

   Mother, my mother.

And what shall the chimes and the bell-ropes play?

One with another.

A weary tune on a weary day,

Mother, my mother.

And what shall be sung for your wedding song?

One with another.

A weary word of a weary wrong,

Mother, my mother.

'The world's way with me runs back,

One with another,

Wedded in white and buried in black,

Mother, my mother.

The world's day and the world's night,

One with another,

Wedded in black and buried in white,

Mother, my mother.

The world's bliss and the world's teen,

    One with another,

It's red for white and it's black for green,

    Mother, my mother.

The world's will and the world's way,

    One with another,

It's sighing for night and crying for day,

    Mother, my mother.

The world's good and the world's worth,

    One with another,

It's earth to flesh and it's flesh to earth,

    Mother, my mother.

    ●   ●   ●   ●   ●   ●

When she came out at the kirkyard gate,

    (One with another)

The bridegroom's mother was there in wait

    (Mother, my mother.)

O mother, where is my great green bed,

    (One with another)

Silk at the foot and gold at the head,

    Mother, my mother ?

Yea, it is ready, the silk and the gold,

    One with another.

But line it well that I lie not cold,

    Mother, my mother.

She laid her cheek to the velvet and vair,

    One with another ;

She laid her arms up under her hair.

    (Mother, my mother.)

Her gold hair fell through her arms fu' low,

    One with another :

Lord God, bring me out of woe !

    (Mother, my mother.)

Her gold hair fell in the gay reeds green,

    One with another :

Lord God, bring me out of teen !

    (Mother, my mother.)

   ●   ●   ●   ●   ●   ●

O mother, where is my lady gone?

    (One with another.)

In the bride-chamber she makes sore moan :

    (Mother, my mother.)

Her hair falls over the velvet and vair,

    (One with another)

Her great soft tears fall over her hair.

    (Mother, my mother.)

When he came into the bride's chamber,

    (One with another)

Her hands were like pale yellow amber.

    (Mother, my mother.)

Her tears made specks in the velvet and vair,

(One with another)

The seeds of the reeds made specks in her hair.

(Mother, my mother.)

He kissed her under the gold on her head ;

(One with another)

The lids of her eyes were like cold lead.

(Mother, my mother.)

He kissed her under the fall of her chin ;

(One with another)

There was right little blood therein.

(Mother, my mother.)

He kissed her under her shoulder sweet;

(One with another)

Her throat was weak, with little heat.

(Mother, my mother.)

He kissed her down by her breast-flowers red,

    One with another ;

They were like river-flowers dead.

    (Mother, my mother.)

What ails you now o' your weeping, wife ?

    (One with another.)

It ails me sair o' my very life.

    (Mother, my mother.)

What ails you now o' your weary ways ?

    (One with another.)

It ails me sair o' my long life-days.

    (Mother, my mother.)

Nay, ye are young, ye are over fair.

    (One with another.)

Though I be young, what needs ye care?

    (Mother, my mother.)

Nay, ye are fair, ye are over sweet.

(One with another.)

Though I be fair, what needs ye greet?

(Mother, my mother.)

Nay, ye are mine while I hold my life.

(One with another.)

O fool, will ye marry the worm for a wife?

(Mother, my mother.)

Nay, ye are mine while I have my breath.

(One with another.)

O fool, will ye marry the dust of death?

(Mother, my mother.)

Yea, ye are mine, we are handfast wed,

One with another.

Nay, I am no man's ; nay, I am dead,

Mother, my mother.

THE WINDS.

O WEARY fa' the east wind,
　And weary fa' the west :
And gin I were under the wan waves wide
　I wot weel wad I rest.

O weary fa' the north wind,
　And weary fa' the south :
The sea went ower my good lord's head
　Or ever he kissed my mouth.

Weary fa' the windward rocks,
　And weary fa' the lee :
They might hae sunken sevenscore ships,
　And let my love's gang free.

And weary fa' ye, mariners a',

And weary fa' the sea :

It might hae taken an hundred men,

And let my ae love be.

A LYKE-WAKE SONG.

FAIR of face, full of pride,
Sit ye down by a dead man's side.

Ye sang songs a' the day :
Sit down at night in the red worm's way.

Proud ye were a' day long :
Ye'll be but lean at evensong.

Ye had gowd kells on your hair :
Nae man kens what ye were.

Ye set scorn by the silken stuff :
Now the grave is clean enough.

Ye set scorn by the rubis ring :

Now the worm is a saft sweet thing

Fine gold and blithe fair face,

Ye are come to a grimly place.

Gold hair and glad grey een,

Nae man kens if ye have been.

A REIVERS NECK-VERSE.

SOME die singing, and some die swinging,
   And weel mot a' they be :
Some die playing, and some die praying,
   And I wot sae winna we, my dear,
   And I wot sae winna we.

Some die sailing, and some die wailing,
   And some die fair and free :
Some die flyting, and some die fighting,
   But I for a fause love's fee, my dear,
   But I for a fause love's fee.

Some die laughing, and some die quaffing,
   And some die high on tree :

Some die spinning, and some die sinning,

But faggot and fire for ye, my dear,

Faggot and fire for ye.

Some die weeping, and some die sleeping,

And some die under sea :

Some die ganging, and some die hanging,

And a twine of a tow for me, my dear,

A twine of a tow for me.

THE WITCH-MOTHER.

'O WHERE will ye gang to and where will ye sleep,
  Against the night begins?'
'My bed is made wi' cauld sorrows,
  My sheets are lined wi' sins.

'And a sair grief sitting at my foot,
  And a sair grief at my head;
And dule to lay me my laigh pillows,
  And teen till I be dead.

'And the rain is sair upon my face,
  And sair upon my hair;
And the wind upon my weary mouth,
  That never may man kiss mair.

'And the snow upon my heavy lips,
   That never shall drink nor eat ;
And shame to cledding, and woe to wedding,
   And pain to drink and meat.

'But woe be to my bairns' father,
   And ever ill fare he :
He has tane a braw bride hame to him,
   Cast out my bairns and me.'

'And what shall they have to their marriage meat
   This day they twain are wed?'
'Meat of strong crying, salt of sad sighing,
   And God restore the dead.'

'And what shall they have to their wedding wine
   This day they twain are wed?'
'Wine of weeping, and draughts of sleeping,
   And God raise up the dead.'

She's tane her to the wild woodside,

   Between the flood and fell :

She's sought a rede against her need

   Of the fiend that bides in hell

She's tane her to the wan burnside,

   She's wrought wi' sang and spell :

She's plighted her soul for doom and dole

   To the fiend that bides in hell.

She's set her young son to her breast,

   Her auld son to her knee :

Says, ' Weel for you the night, bairnies,

   And weel the morn for me.'

She looked fu' lang in their een, sighing,

   And sair and sair grat she :

She has slain her young son at her breast,

   Her auld son at her knee.

She's sodden their flesh wi' saft water,

    She's mixed their blood with wine :

She's tane her to the braw bride-house,

    Where a' were boun' to dine.

She poured the red wine in his cup,

    And his een grew fain to greet :

She set the baked meats at his hand,

    And bade him drink and eat.

Says, 'Eat your fill of your flesh, my lord,

    And drink your fill of your wine,

For a' thing's yours and only yours

    That has been yours and mine.'

Says, 'Drink your fill of your wine, my lord,

    And eat your fill of your bread :

I would they were quick in my body again,

    Or I that bare them dead'

He struck her head frae her fair body,

  And dead for grief he fell :

And there were twae mair sangs in heaven

  And twae mair sauls in hell.

THE BRIDE'S TRAGEDY.

'THE wind wears roun', the day wears doun,
   The moon is grisly grey ;
There's nae man rides by the mirk muirsides,
   Nor down the dark Tyne's way.'
     In, in, out and in,
      Blaws the wind and whirls the whin.

'And winna ye watch the night wi' me,
   And winna ye wake the morn?
Foul shame it were that your ae mither
   Should brook her ae son's scorn.'
     In, in, out and in,
      Blaws the wind and whirls the whin.

'O mither, I may not sleep nor stay,

  My weird is ill to dree ;

For a fause faint lord of the south seaboard

  Wad win my bride of me.'

    In, in, out and in,

    Blaws the wind and whirls the whin.

'The winds are strang, and the nights are lang,

  And the ways are sair to ride :

And I maun gang to wreak my wrang,

  And ye maun bide and bide.'

    In, in, out and in,

    Blaws the wind and whirls the whin.

'Gin I maun bide and bide, Willie,

  I wot my weird is sair :

Weel may ye get ye a light love yet,

  But never a mither mair.'

    In, in, out and in,

    Blaws the wind and whirls the whin.

'O gin the morrow be great wi' sorrow,

    The wyte be yours of a' :

But though ye slay me that haud and stay me,

    The weird ye will maun fa'.'

        In, in, out and in,

        Blaws the wind and whirls the whin.

When cocks were crawing and day was dawing,

    He's boun' him forth to ride :

And the ae first may he's met that day

    Was fause Earl Robert's bride.

        In, in, out and in,

        Blaws the wind and whirls the whin.

O blithe and braw were the bride-folk a',

    But sad and saft rade she ;

And sad as doom was her fause bridegroom,

    But fair and fain was he.

        In, in, out and in,

        Blaws the wind and whirls the whin.

'And winna ye bide, sae saft ye ride,

   And winna ye speak wi' me ?

For mony's the word and the kindly word

   I have spoken aft wi' thee.'

     In, in, out and in,

     Blaws the wind and whirls the whin.

'My lamp was lit yestreen, Willie,

   My window-gate was wide :

But ye camena nigh me till day came by me

   And made me not your bride.'

     In, in, out and in,

     Blaws the wind and whirls the whin.

He's set his hand to her bridle-rein,

   He's turned her horse away :

And the cry was sair, and the wrath was mair,

   And fast and fain rode they.

     In, in, out and in,

     Blaws the wind and whirls the whin.

But when they came by Chollerford,

I wot the ways were fell ;

For broad and brown the spate swang down,

And the lift was mirk as hell.

In, in, out and in,

Blaws the wind and whirls the whin.

'And will ye ride yon fell water,

Or will ye bide for fear ?

Nae scathe ye'll win o' your father's kin,

Though they should slay me here.'

In, in, out and in,

Blaws the wind and whirls the whin.

'I had liefer ride yon fell water,

Though strange it be to ride,

Than I wad stand on the fair green strand

And thou be slain beside.'

In, in, out and in,

Blaws the wind and whirls the whin.

' I had liefer swim yon wild water,

    Though sair it be to bide,

Than I wad stand at a strange man's hand,

    To be a strange man's bride.'

      In, in, out and in,

      Blaws the wind and whirls the whin.

' I had liefer drink yon dark water,

    Wi' the stanes to make my bed,

And the faem to hide me, and thou beside me,

    Than I wad see thee dead.'

      In, in, out and in,

      Blaws the wind and whirls the whin.

He's kissed her twice, he's kissed her thrice,

    On cheek and lip and chin :

He's wound her rein to his hand again,

    And lightly they leapt in.

      In, in, out and in,

      Blaws the wind and whirls the whin.

Their hearts were high to live or die,

Their steeds were stark of limb :

But the stream was starker, the spate was darker,

Than man might live and swim.

In, in, out and in,

Blaws the wind and whirls the whin.

The first ae step they strode therein,

It smote them foot and knee :

But ere they wan to the mid water

The spate was as the sea.

In, in, out and in,

Blaws the wind and whirls the whin.

But when they wan to the mid water,

It smote them hand and head :

And nae man knows but the wave that flows

Where they lie drowned and dead.

In, in, out and in,

Blaws the wind and whirls the whin.

A JACOBITE'S FAREWELL.

1716.

THERE'S nae mair lands to tyne, my dear,
  And nae mair lives to gie :
Though a man think sair to live nae mair,
  There's but one day to die

For a' things come and a' days gane,
  What needs ye rend your hair ?
But kiss me till the morn's morrow,
  Then I'll kiss ye nae mair.

O lands are lost and life's losing,
  And what were they to gie ?
Fu' mony a man gives all he can,
  But nae man else gives ye.

Our king wons ower the sea's water,

And I in prison sair :

But I'll win out the morn's morrow,

And ye'll see me nae mair

A JACOBITE'S EXILE.

1746.

THE weary day rins down and dies,

The weary night wears through :

And never an hour is fair wi' flower,

And never a flower wi' dew.

I would the day were night for me,

I would the night were day :

For then would I stand in my ain fair land,

As now in dreams I may.

O lordly flow the Loire and Seine,

And loud the dark Durance :

But bonnier shine the braes of Tyne

Than a' the fields of France ;

And the waves of Till that speak sae still

Gleam goodlier where they glance.

O weel were they that fell fighting

On dark Drumossie's day:

They keep their hame ayont the faem,

And we die far away.

O sound they sleep, and saft, and deep,

But night and day wake we ;

And ever between the sea-banks green

Sounds loud the sundering sea.

And ill we sleep, sae sair we weep,

But sweet and fast sleep they ;

And the mool that haps them roun' and laps them

Is e'en their country's clay;

But the land we tread that are not dead

Is strange as night by day.

Strange as night in a strange man's sight,

    Though fair as dawn it be:

For what is here that a stranger's cheer

    Should yet wax blithe to see?

The hills stand steep, the dells lie deep,

    The fields are green and gold:

The hill-streams sing, and the hill-sides ring,

    As ours at home of old.

But hills and flowers are nane of ours,

    And ours are oversea:

And the kind strange land whereon we stand,

    It wotsna what were we

Or ever we came, wi' scathe and shame,

    To try what end might be.

Scathe, and shame, and a waefu' name,

    And a weary time and strange,

Have they that seeing a weird for dreeing

    Can die, and cannot change.

Shame and scorn may we thole that mourn,

   Though sair be they to dree :

But ill may we bide the thoughts we hide,

   Mair keen than wind and sea.

Ill may we thole the night's watches,

   And ill the weary day :

And the dreams that keep the gates of sleep,

   A waefu' gift gie they ;

For the sangs they sing us, the sights they bring us,

   The morn blaws all away.

On Aikenshaw the sun blinks braw,

   The burn rins blithe and fain :

There's nought wi' me I wadna gie

   To look thereon again.

On Keilder-side the wind blaws wide ;

   There sounds nae hunting-horn

That rings sae sweet as the winds that beat

   Round banks where Tyne is born.

The Wansbeck sings with all her springs,

   The bents and braes give ear ;

But the wood that rings wi' the sang she sings

   I may not see nor hear;

For far and far thae blithe burns are,

   And strange is a' thing near.

The light there lightens, the day there brightens,

   The loud wind there lives free :

Nae light comes nigh me or wind blaws by me

   That I wad hear or see.

But O gin I were there again,

   Afar ayont the faem,

Cauld and dead in the sweet saft bed

   That haps my sires at hame !

We'll see nae mair the sea-banks fair,

   And the sweet grey gleaming sky,

And the lordly strand of Northumberland,

And the goodly towers thereby :

And none shall know but the winds that blow

The graves wherein we lie.

THE TYNESIDE WIDOW.

THERE's mony a man loves land and life,

    Loves life and land and fee ;

And mony a man loves fair women,

    But never a man loves me, my love,

    But never a man loves me.

O weel and weel for a' lovers,

    I wot weel may they be ;

And weel and weel for a' fair maidens,

    But aye mair woe for me, my love,

    But aye mair woe for me.

O weel be wi' you, ye sma' flowers,

    Ye flowers and every tree ;

And weel be wi' you, a' birdies,

But teen and tears wi' me, my love,

But teen and tears wi' me.

O weel be yours, my three brethren,

And ever weel be ye ;

Wi' deeds for doing and loves for wooing,

But never a love for me, my love,

But never a love for me.

And weel be yours, my seven sisters,

And good love-days to see,

And long life-days and true lovers,

But never a day for me, my love,

But never a day for me.

Good times wi' you, ye bauld riders,

By the hieland and the lee ;

And by the leeland and by the hieland

It's weary times wi' me, my love,

It's weary times wi' me.

Good days wi' you, ye good sailors,

  Sail in and out the sea ;

And by the beaches and by the reaches

  It's heavy days wi' me, my love,

  It's heavy days wi' me.

I had his kiss upon my mouth,

  His bairn upon my knee ;

I would my soul and body were twain,

  And the bairn and the kiss wi' me, my love,

  And the bairn and the kiss wi' me.

The bairn down in the mools, my dear,

  O saft and saft lies she ;

I would the mools were ower my head,

  And the young bairn fast wi' me, my love,

  And the young bairn fast wi' me.

The father under the faem, my dear,

  O sound and sound sleeps he ;

I would the faem were ower my face,

　　And the father lay by me, my love,

　　And the father lay by me.

I would the faem were ower my face,

　　Or the mools on my ee-bree ;

And waking-time with a' lovers,

　　But sleeping-time wi' me, my love,

　　But sleeping-time wi' me.

I would the mools were meat in my mouth,

　　The saut faem in my ee ;

And the land-worm and the water-worm

　　To feed fu' sweet on me, my love,

　　To feed fu' sweet on me.

My life is sealed with a seal of love,

　　And locked with love for a key ;

And I lie wrang and I wake lang,

　　But ye tak' nae thought for me, my love,

　　But ye tak' nae thought for me.

We were weel fain of love, my dear,

  O fain and fain were we ;

It was weel with a' the weary world,

  But O, sae weel wi' me, my love,

  But O, sae weel wi' me.

We were nane ower mony to sleep, my dear,

  I wot we were but three ;

And never a bed in the weary world

  For my bairn and my dear and me, my love,

  For my bairn and my dear and me.

DEDICATION.

THE years are many, the changes more,
Since wind and sun on the wild sweet shore
  Where Joyous Gard stands stark by the sea
With face as bright as in years of yore

Shone, swept, and sounded, and laughed for glee
More deep than a man's or a child's may be,
  On a day when summer was wild and glad,
And the guests of the wind and the sun were we.

The light that lightens from seasons clad
With darkness now, is it glad or sad?
  Not sad but glad should it shine, meseems,
On eyes yet fain of the joy they had.

For joy was there with us ; joy that gleams

And murmurs yet in.the world of dreams

    Where thought holds fast, as a constant warder,

The days when I rode by moors and streams,

Reining my rhymes into buoyant order

Through honied leagues of the northland border.

    Though thought or memory fade, and prove

A faithless keeper, a thriftless hoarder,

One landmark never can change remove,

One sign can the years efface not.   Love,

    More strong than death or than doubt may be,

Treads down their strengths, and abides above.

Yea, change and death are his servants : we,

Whom love of the dead links fast, though free.

    May smile as they that beheld the dove

Bear home her signal across the sea.

PRINTED BY
SPOTTISWOODE AND CO. LTD., LONDON
COLCHESTER AND ETON